DO NOT REMOVE
CARDS FROM POCKET

THE WAY HOME

FARRAR, STRAUS & GIROUX

NEW YORK

THE

WAY HOME

Leigh Sauerwein

PICTURES BY MILES HYMAN

Text copyright © 1994 by Leigh Sauerwein
Art copyright © 1994 by Miles Hyman
All rights reserved
Originally published in French translation as
Sur l'autre rive by Editions Gallimard, 1992
Published simultaneously in Canada by HarperCollinsCanadaLtd
Printed in the United States of America
Designed by Cynthia Krupat
First American edition, 1994

Library of Congress Cataloging-in-Publication Data
Sauerwein, Leigh.
The way home / Leigh Sauerwein ; pictures by Miles Hyman. — 1st
American ed.
p. cm.
Summary: A collection of short stories capturing moments in the
American West, from 1853 to 1992.
1. West (U.S.)—Juvenile fiction. 2. Frontier and pioneer life—
West (U.S.)—Juvenile fiction. 3. Children's stories, American.
[1. West (U.S.)—Fiction. 2. Frontier and pioneer life—West
(U.S.)—Fiction. 3. Short stories.]   I. Hyman, Miles, ill.
II. Title.
PZ7.S2503Way 1993   [Fic]—dc20   93-10097 CIP AC

For Laurent, Julie,
Olivia, and David

Contents

1989

Storm

Warning

Ever since he was ten years old, people in Beaver Creek had seen Joseph Budd riding his bike out to Jonathan Walking Bear's hamburger stand. The Indian had built it cleverly from a trailer and it stood, a few yards back from the road, two miles out of town, out where the cornfields gave way to the prairie. When Joe turned twelve, Jonathan had not yet taken the wheels off the trailer and he kept his '76 Ford pickup truck in good condition: "Just in case I decide to move, take a trip or something," he always said.

Jonathan had done a lot of traveling.

Joe's mother, Margaret Rachel, let him go and visit Jonathan Walking Bear just about whenever he felt like it. She let him dash out of the neat red brick house on Sorrel Road with the flowered sofa and the spotless kitchen and ride out of the little white-steepled town all the way to Jonathan's.

"How come you let Joe go out there all the time?" asked her neighbor every few days, a stout, fluttery woman with pink cheeks. "He spends more time with that crazy Indian than he does with you!"

But Rachel usually replied gently, "They get along. It won't hurt him. With his father gone, the boy needs a man's companionship."

Rachel Budd had married back East the summer after her last year in college. Everyone had heard about the man's tragic death six months later and how she had gone to stay with her grandmother in Vermont till her baby was born. When she returned to Beaver Creek, she had a ring on her finger and a black-haired, blue-eyed child in her arms—"the spitting image of his mama," people said. And she had stayed on.

There had been no more talk of leaving the little town for a better life in some big city. She took the job at the post office and moved back into her Aunt Tilly's red brick house on Sorrel Road where she had grown up.

Everyone watched her with the boy and after a while they said she was a good mother, and there was never any gossip about her. She lived quietly with her son. No one questioned her right to give him her name. He grew up Joseph Budd.

And so, when Rachel Budd said there was no harm in letting Joe ride out to Jonathan Walking Bear's place, that was that.

Why Jonathan had come back to Beaver Creek to set up a hamburger stand in the middle of nowhere, nobody knew except Jonathan. But the hamburgers were so good people were willing to drive the two miles out of town to buy them. He put herbs and sweet spices in the meat and served a special hot sauce he wouldn't tell anyone about.

"It's a South American recipe" was all he would ever say in his low, quiet voice.

"Mexican, Jonathan?" people would ask. "I bet it's Mexican—you lived down there for a while after you got back from Vietnam, didn't you?"

But Jonathan just clammed up. There was no point in trying to get Jonathan to talk when he had decided to be silent.

The boy knew that, too.

Jonathan was a tall, lean man of forty-five. He wore his slightly graying hair in braids, old Indian style.

"Hey, Jonathan, where's your war paint?" some people would yell from their cars, waiting on their orders.

It was like a game they played every time they came out to the trailer.

"Hey, Jonathan, when you gonna get a haircut?"

When Jonathan brought out the square white boxes with the burgers still sizzling inside their rolls, sometimes he would answer them quietly, saying, "I'm pure Sioux except for my great-great-great-grandmother, who was a white girl. She ran off with a young warrior when she was sixteen. I'm Lakota and I wear my hair the way I want it, Lakota style!"

Sometimes he would just look at the people with disdain, and say, "Immigrants!"

Joe loved that. He would howl with laughter from behind the counter. He liked to come out and give Jonathan a hand on weekends when business was heaviest, flipping the burgers on the little gas grill, then slipping them into the waiting buns.

But sometimes the trailer was shut up tight for days at a time and the pickup truck was gone. That usually meant Jonathan had taken a trip to Silver City. When he got back, he always looked tired and sad. It was never a good idea to have a conversation with Jonathan on those days.

Joe would ask questions anyway:

"What do you do over there in Silver City?"

"Gamble and drink and pick up girls."

"Do you have any fun?"

"No."

"Why do you do it, then?"

"It takes my mind off my troubles."

"What are your troubles, Jonathan?"

"I'd just as soon not talk about that."

But some days Jonathan would look at the boy as if he were seeing something far away, and the stories would come. Joe watched and waited for those times like a fox watches and waits for its prey.

They would settle down into Jonathan's tiny room at one end of the trailer. Joe would sprawl on the one old tattered armchair and Jonathan would stretch out on the bed and light his pipe. Trump, Jonathan's lopsided yellow dog, would come in last and thump down on the cheap piece of blue carpet glued to the floor.

The best stories were always about Crazy Horse, the greatest of the Sioux warriors. Crazy Horse, *Tasunke Witco*, the light-haired boy, the one they called Curly when he was a child, the one who was always by himself, the one the Sioux called Our Strange Man, the one who defeated the great General Crook at the battle of the Rosebud.

Crazy Horse, who was at the head of the attack that rubbed out Long Hair, General Custer, at Little Big Horn, who went into battle with hailstones painted on his body, a small brown stone tied under his left arm. Crazy Horse, *Tasunke Witco*, Hoka Hey!

And sometimes Jonathan told Joe how Little Big Horn had lasted about as long as it takes for a hungry man to eat his dinner, and how the dust from the horses' hooves had blocked out the light of the sun that day, and how bullets and arrows vanished before they could touch Crazy Horse, and how no white man ever took a photograph of him, and how, after his dying, closed up in a white man's dead wood house, they took his body away into the Badlands where no one ever, ever found his grave. Crazy Horse, *Tasunke Witco*, Hoka Hey!

In the summer afternoons, the boy would ride home, often repeating the words he had learned from Jonathan in Sioux. As he pedaled faster and faster, he sang to himself: "Hoka Hey, Tasunke Witco." He especially liked the sound of those words. They made him feel strong. "Tasunke Witco, Hoka Hey!"

Rachel worked at the post office, sorting the afternoon mail, slipping the letters into the cubbyholes. It was very hot this year. Even for Nebraska. Even for August. The fan didn't help much. When would they decide to put in air-conditioning? Maybe she would stop at the vegetable stand on her way home and pick up some squash. And a watermelon. The boy would like that, she thought. He would flash her his brilliant smile, the smile that made her heart rise and her burden seem light.

The letters flew from her quick hands into their cubbyholes. Baker, Burton, Curtis, Chadwick, Coleman . . . I've raised him up alone, she thought. Half of her felt proud, but the rest, hidden in a dark place somewhere deep down, felt frightened and sad.

Suddenly she missed Tilly. Her mother's sister. Aunt Mathilda Linstrum, who had taken her in, a child of three, without a murmur after the automobile accident that killed her parents. It was so far away now. She couldn't even remember her mother's face. But she remembered Tilly with a stab of pain. The small bent figure, the sweet high voice, the bright eyes, and the quick steps in the kitchen, on the stairs: Margaret Rachel! Have you done your homework? Have you?

Tilly, who never married because no man wanted to marry a little hunchbacked woman. Tilly, who took her to concerts and to her first rodeo. Tilly, who made her be home by ten until she was over seventeen.

"Hoka Hey!" yelled the boy, kicking open the screen door of the post office, hoping to make his mother jump. "You know what that means?

It's a Sioux battle cry. You know what the Sioux sang when they went into battle?"

He had run all his sentences together without stopping.

She smiled and said, "No, what?"

He paused dramatically. "They sang, 'It's a good day to die!' "

The ceiling fan stirred the warm air. Somewhere across the adjacent cornfield, a dog barked.

"I know," said his mother quietly.

The boy turned and looked at her. "You do?" he asked incredulously. And then, almost accusingly: "How do you know?"

Rachel laughed. "Anyone who knows a little bit about the Sioux has heard about that war cry," she answered. "It's famous. People know about it way over in Europe. In Japan even. You aren't the only one."

"You're kidding," said the boy.

"Certainly not," said Rachel with a laugh that showed her pretty white teeth. "Let's go home now."

"You mean you know all about Crazy Horse and Red Cloud and Sitting Bull and Kicking Bear . . ."

"I know a little bit about them, yes. Come on, Joe, put your bike in the trunk and we'll stop off at the vegetable stand before it closes."

———

"How's Jonathan?" she asked at dinner.

"Oh, he's okay. He hasn't gone to Silver City for a while, so he looks okay. Sometimes when he gets back from Silver City he looks half dead."

After a while, she said, "You tell him to keep away from that place."

The boy looked up, surprised. "Oh, I do, Mom. Every time. He knows it's bad for him. But sometimes he says he needs to forget things. So he goes to Silver City."

"How come you never come out to Jonathan's?" asked Joe as they cleared the table together. "You came out the first time. You used to be friends, didn't you?"

"That was a long time ago. Before you were born."

She fell silent.

"Talk to me, Mom!"

"Jonathan went to Vietnam. The war did bad things to him. Very bad things. When he came home, he was on drugs. I didn't want to see him like that. He had gone kind of crazy. So we lost touch. Now that he's back, I'm glad you're friends."

"You sound like a telegram."

"I don't enjoy talking about that particular subject, if you don't mind."

Flopping back on the flowery cushions, the boy laid his head on his mother's lap. Absent-mindedly, she ran her fingers across his forehead and through his dark hair, slowly, gently, as the light faded, the evening ritual before sleep.

And the ritual question which was never long in coming. "Tell me about my father. What was he like?"

She would always answer the question in her quiet way, bringing the dead man carefully back to life, describing his face, his beautiful dark eyes, and saying how brilliant he had been and what a great scientist he would have become and the happiness she had known during their short life together.

But tonight her voice sounded tired.

And the boy went to bed filled with a sense of longing and emptiness. He felt the ghost of his father standing over him, watching him. Sleep didn't come to him for a long time.

"Did I ever tell you how Geronimo got his name?" asked Jonathan.

It was Monday and they had walked out to a high grassy bluff overlooking the prairie about a mile and a half behind the trailer. Now they were stretched out in the grass under the late-afternoon sun.

"Tell me, Jonathan!" Joe loved Apache stories because they were always fierce, like a burning desert wind.

"Well, when old Geronimo was born way up in the mountains somewhere between Arizona and New Mexico, when he was just another fat little Apache baby crawling around in the dust, his mother and father called him Goyahkla. You know what that means?"

"No, what?"

"It means 'the one who yawns'! 'the yawner'! Well, his parents couldn't have made a bigger mistake with that name, when you think of what that little baby's destiny was to be."

The boy began to travel on Jonathan's words, making one of the journeys through Geronimo's life. It was like a familiar path, yet always exciting to follow.

"The Apache were trading down in Mexico at a place they called Kas-ki-yeh. The men had all gone into the town. Only the women and children and a few old warriors had stayed in the camp along the river.

"Goyahkla's mother was there, and his young wife, Alope, with their baby. Children were playing in the river, splashing each other and jumping up and down. But all of a sudden a very strange silence fell upon the place. Even the birds stopped singing in the trees.

"It was then that the people saw the soldiers. They were on horseback, motionless, on the ridge above the camp. Slowly one of them drew his sword. It glinted an instant in the sunlight like an evil smile. And then they charged. They flew down on the camp like wolves. Not many survived. Goyahkla lost his whole family—wife, mother, and child.

"Goyahkla just about went crazy after that. He went back into the mountains with his people. He turned mean, ill-tempered; no one could speak to him. After a while, his face came to look something like a falcon's, like a bird of prey. He was burning up inside. Then slowly he began to plan his revenge. Time didn't mean a thing.

"It took him about a year to gather a war party from the different Apache bands. He was no great speaker like Cochise, but he had lost so much that when he told his story, his words had power. Warriors followed him. When he had enough men, they traveled down into Mexico. On foot through the mountains, down to the town where the soldiers were.

"When they got there, they just waited outside the town on a little rise with a forest at their backs. Of course, only a few warriors could be seen, standing still as statues. The others were hidden in the trees. That was Goyahkla's idea. They just waited for the soldiers to come out after them.

"After a day or so, the soldiers had to come out to attack them. When they finally decided to come out of the town to fight, it was September 30, Saint Jerome's day, San Gerónimo in Spanish, because in the Catholic calendar every day has the name of a saint.

"Well, out they marched right into Goyahkla's trap. Because he had his warriors hidden in a wide U-shape, behind the trees. When the Mexicans were well inside the 'U,' all hell broke loose.

"It was quite a fight. And right in the middle of the battle, someone started shouting 'Geronimo! Geronimo!' It was probably a soldier calling on the saint at the top of his voice, shouting a prayer in Spanish to the saint to save them from the fierce Apache warriors, whose arrows and bullets never seemed to miss. But they were defeated. That night, the Apache moved out in silence and disappeared into the mountains.

"And sometime, in the darkness of that night, Goyahkla knew that his old name had fallen from him like the skin from a snake. He knew his new name had to be the cry that had echoed over the battlefield. He became Geronimo . . ."

———

After a while, Joe smelled the grass again and heard the wind running through it. Jonathan was smoking his pipe, his eyes turned toward the horizon. From this place on the bluff, it was like gazing out to sea.

Joe looked at his friend, the long legs in jeans, the tennis shoes, the soft worn blue cotton shirt, the graying hair. "How come you never tell any stories about the Vietnam War?" he asked.

Jonathan was silent. Joe thought he was going to refuse to answer the question. He was going to clam up; it would be like the hot sauce.

But finally he just said very quietly, with the pipe between his teeth, "You wouldn't want to hear about that."

"Jonathan," said the boy after a while.

"What?"

"Jonathan, I . . ."

"What is it?"

"What would you do if you thought someone wasn't telling you the truth about something?"

Jonathan lay back in the grass and watched the sky for a long time. Then he said, speaking slowly and carefully, "In the old days, when an Indian wanted to know something, the answer to a mystery, the solution to a problem, or just how to act in a certain situation, he would ask the Great Spirit, Tunkasila, or the spirits of the earth to send him a vision."

"A vision? How?"

"Well, a man would go out somewhere alone, preferably up on a hill. And he would clear a square space of whatever was growing there. Then he would sink four poles in the ground, toward each of the four directions, north, west, south, and east. And he would send a prayer to each of these great directions which to him were all things. And then he would just stay up there without eating or drinking."

"For how long?"

"Well, as long as it took for the vision to come to him."

"And how long did that take?"

"Sometimes two, three days. Sometimes it didn't come at all."

"How did they know when it came?"

"Well, it could be an animal, or a sound. Sometimes it could come in a dream.

"Of course, they didn't always understand the experience. That's why the Sioux had their seers, men who were close to the spirits and could interpret the spirit messages . . . But sometimes you understand right away what a vision is saying to you. Then it is like a seed you plant in your soul."

"Did you ever have a vision, Jonathan?" asked the boy.

Rachel did the shopping, pushing the big cart up one aisle and down the other. Mindlessly, she pulled boxes and cans off the shelves and laid them in the cart. It was nice to be in the air-conditioned supermarket. There would be no time today to stop by the vegetable stand. She selected some grapes and a chicken for roasting.

She advanced as in a dream. Soon the boy would be coming home. She saw him running from the bluff with Trump, the Indian walking a few steps behind them with his long, rhythmic strides, watching them with his careful dark eyes. Then she could see her son shaking hands with the man. She saw him hurl a last stick for the dog, then pedal down the flat road, prairie stretching out to the right and to the left of him, then corn, then wheat, then the town.

The scene began again. They were walking toward her from the bluff—the tall man, the boy, and the dog. She was standing beside the trailer, looking out over the prairie. They were coming back; they would soon be home.

"Sometimes I have a vision," said Jonathan. "It comes to me in a dream. I'm way out on the prairie and I see a young Indian woman running along this bluff. Then, up against the clouds, a big bird appears. I see it is a golden eagle. The eagle swoops down on her, faster and faster, closer and closer, and just barely grazes her uplifted face with one wing. Then it soars up again, very high. She runs along the bluff with her arms outstretched, her face lifted to the sky. She shouts for joy and the eagle swoops down again. It's like a game they are playing. Sometimes they both cry out together under the wind. It seems to go on and on. I never saw anything so beautiful. Afterwards, it's like being made clean, it's like being full of some light that I can't see, but I can feel it. The eagle woman, she carries away my sorrows."

He paused. "Then I don't have the bad dreams, the war dreams and all the rest."

Joe looked up, alerted by something in the man's voice. Jonathan was leaning forward, his face hidden in his hands. Joe reached out and touched his shoulder. Then the man wept, rocking back and forth, tears spilling over his fingers. Joe was frightened, but he kept his hand on Jonathan's shoulder. He kept saying "It's okay, Jonathan, it's going to be okay," because he couldn't think of anything else to say.

After a while, they got up and walked back to the trailer, side by side. Jonathan didn't speak of the incident again, but when they shook hands he said, "You're a good boy, Joe. You will grow up to be a fine man."

"What do you mean? You talk as if we weren't going to see each other again," said Joe.

"It's time for me to move on. This old trailer has been sitting here long enough. I've got some traveling to do. My hanging-around days are over."

"You mean you're going to leave town?"

"Right now I've got some deliveries to make. Throw your bike in the back of the truck; I'll drive you home. There's a big demand out for my hot sauce these days."

Lots of people had ordered Jonathan's hot sauce, which he delivered in old ketchup bottles, sterilized and neatly capped. "It will keep in the refrigerator for three months," he said, repeating the same phrase to everyone in his taciturn way.

The mayor's wife bought two. Joe sat in the back of the truck parked on the tree-lined street while Jonathan walked up to the door of the big Victorian frame house and handed the bottles to her in a brown paper bag. She was a tall blond woman from Texas and declared authoritatively that Jonathan's was the best hot sauce she had ever encountered. Her voice was loud and twangy; Joe could hear her clearly from the truck.

"You leave town without giving me that recipe and I'll send the police after you!" she called playfully as Jonathan walked back toward the truck. He lifted one arm without looking back.

When they swung into Joe's driveway, Jonathan kept the motor running.

"You want to come in for a minute?" asked the boy.

"No, don't bother about me. I've got to run."

"I bet Mom has some cold lemonade waiting."

"No, thanks."

"You aren't leaving yet, are you?"

"I'll tell you when I go. It won't be long."

Rachel heard their voices, but when she came out on the porch, the pickup truck was already halfway down the street. She watched it disappear around the corner of Sorrel and Elm.

"Jonathan says he's leaving town," said the boy.

"Leaving?" Her voice was very low.

"He says he'll let me know but that it won't be long. He says his hanging-around days are over. I guess he just can't stay long in one place."

"Some men are like that," said his mother and walked quickly back into the house.

That night the boy slept badly again. He woke up several times. When he realized that sleep would not come, he got up and walked to his open window. The heat of the day was still palpable, in spite of the darkness. There was no wind. The stars were very bright. He leaned on the windowsill, running his fingers along the familiar lines of the cracked paint, pushing his forehead against the screen. He watched the sky, hoping to see a shooting star, and listened to the night sounds until his arms cramped and his eyes began to close again.

When Joe rode out to the trailer early the next morning, he found it was shut up tight and Jonathan was nowhere in sight. But the pickup truck was there. Then he heard Trump whining from inside the trailer. He opened the door. Trump dashed out as if he had been cooped up for hours. Joe stepped up into the little room.

The whisky bottle on the small table was almost empty. There were crushed beer cans on the floor. Jonathan was lying on the bed, breathing heavily. He was on his back, his long hands at his sides, seemingly lifeless.

"Jonathan," the boy called, shaking him by the shoulder. "Jonathan!"

The man rolled over. He moaned almost like a child. He was lost in sleep. The boy felt betrayed, as if Jonathan had already left him forever. Now they would never go hunting together. None of the great promises would come true. The long leather rifle case with the silver handle would stay under the bed and gather dust. And then Jonathan would go away. It

would all be over. He would grow up without his friend.

He went out and sat on the steps leading up to the trailer door. He left the door slightly open, so he could hear. Trump came back from relieving himself and flopped in the dust at his feet. They waited there together. The heat was suffocating.

Suddenly the boy got up, turned on his heel, and walked out across the prairie toward the bluff. When he reached the top, half an hour later, he began the job he had set for himself. Slowly, methodically, he began tearing out the whispering grass to make a bare space. Suddenly he felt as if he was ripping Jonathan's stories up out of the ground. But he kept on pulling. It took a long time. Beads of sweat rolled down his face, but he kept on pulling up the grasses. Finally he had cleared a space about one yard square. Not knowing exactly how to proceed, he rose awkwardly and faced the north, then the west, then the east, and then the south, remaining in each position for several minutes before turning.

Jonathan had said, "They prayed to the great directions which were all things to them." Joe sat down in the square and looked out to the horizon. The heat was rising. He realized suddenly he had eaten no breakfast. He kept looking out at the horizon, a hundred miles away.

Jonathan was walking the dark jungle path through the fiery wet heat. The dead woman was lying a few yards ahead; she was lying across the path like a broken doll. Her dress was a dull red. It reminded him suddenly of Carl Linstrum's big red barn, out on the ranch where he used to work. The first guy to reach her bent down to move the body. Jonathan screamed, "Don't touch her!" But it was too late. The explosion from the hidden bomb tore the young man apart. Then Jonathan was running through high grass. Running faster and faster. He heard the steady beating of a helicopter overhead. But it didn't come down. Then he was on the dark path once more and the dream began again . . .

Rachel found the boy's hastily scribbled note on the kitchen table. "Gone to see Jonathan. Love, Joe."

Later, at the post office, she tried to keep her mind on her work. The fan was humming. Periodically, a gust of warm air ran over her face. She tried not to think back to the day when she had seen Jonathan for the first time, when Tilly had taken her to the rodeo.

The sudden streak of shining black hair, the left arm flailing high, the perfect balance of the long, slim body, moving with the wildly bucking horse, as if he and the horse were one body. She had never seen anyone ride like that.

Somebody in the crowd behind them had said, "That's Jonathan Walking Bear. He works at Carl Linstrum's ranch out by Sweet Springs."

She knew then she would see him again, because Tilly would want to say hello to Carl after the rodeo.

They were serving cold lemonade behind the stalls after the cow roping. He was standing with his back turned, facing one of the roping horses; he looked as if he were talking to it. Big, jovial Carl Linstrum had hollered, "Jonathan, come on over here!"

Turning to Tilly, he joked, "This boy's my Indian cowboy, best damn bronco buster in the state."

He had walked up, his face covered with dust. He was still wearing the leather chaps over his jeans.

"Jonathan, I want you to meet my cousin, Mathilda Linstrum. And this is Margaret Rachel, her niece."

He looked older up close. He was twenty-eight that year. She had just turned seventeen.

She remembered the tiny wrinkles around his eyes. He nodded without smiling, first looking at Tilly, then at her.

Carl handed him a glass of lemonade. "Drink this down, Jonathan, my man," he said. "If anybody deserves it, you do!"

He gulped down the clear liquid, the ice tinkling against the glass as he drank. He wiped his mouth on his sleeve. "Hope you ladies enjoyed the rodeo." He seemed to pause ever so slightly; then he nodded again and moved away.

People came into the post office to buy stamps, to send packages and registered letters. Rachel went through the motions automatically. Her face was calm. Her thick dark hair was carefully tied back in a ponytail. Her hands worked efficiently. No one could know what was going on inside her. She smiled, she thanked, she made small talk, asked about babies. She wished everyone a nice day. She was good at that, good at hiding her feelings, good at hiding from herself, too. Good at forgetting, pushing down what rose to trouble the smooth waters of her life.

The post office was quiet again. She was alone. She closed her eyes.

After that day at the rodeo, she had started

going out to Carl's place, out to Sweet Springs, out to the ranch.

"I want to do some riding again," she had said to Tilly.

Carl was glad to see her return. "Well, if it isn't Miss Rachel! Think you can still get up on a horse?"

She and Jonathan would ride for hours along the river. The memory of those days washed over her. She couldn't stop the waves. He always stayed a few paces behind her. She could hear the sound of his horse at her back. They almost never spoke. Just being near him was enough for her. She waited for the moment when, sometimes, he would give her his hand to help her down.

She could hear him saying, "When the light on us was clear, we were a great people." And the time they had left the horses tied to a cottonwood and he had walked into the falling dusk along the river and she had followed him into the darkness and he had spoken without seeming to see her as the water ran by them: "We always knew about the earth. We knew everything these fools are just figuring out with their theories and their stiff talk about the planet. We knew it from the beginning. The earth is alive like a mother. And the sky overhead like a father, and everything between them."

And she remembered at last how they had found each other lying in the grass. And the good smell of him and the sound of their voices together, rising and falling.

Tilly had seen through her right away.

"I know you're seeing that Jonathan. You listen to me, Margaret Rachel Budd, he's nothing but a ranch hand. And on top of it, he's a grown man! Do you want to ruin your life? You stay away from Sweet Springs from now on. Do you hear me?!"

But somewhere under Tilly's indignant little voice she had felt her aunt drinking and breathing up the love she felt.

And then, suddenly, Tilly had died. Quietly, as if she had wilted. There had been a lot of people at the church. Rachel sat in the white wooden pew with Grandma Budd, who had come all the way from Vermont for the memorial service. She sat in the white wooden pew, listening to the organ music and the droning voice of the preacher, not feeling anything. Like a severed limb with no nerves.

"I want you to come and stay with me for a while, Rachel," Grandma Budd had said later at the house in her deep, strong voice. "You need to see new places, meet different people." She understood suddenly from her grandmother's tone that the old woman didn't like Nebraska, didn't like the little town she had grown up in, and possibly had not liked her mother, a farm girl, a hick, a person to be looked down upon.

"Don't go, Rachel," he had said. "Stay with me. I'll take care of you." They were sitting by the river. The wind made ripples on the water. As always, he hadn't said much else.

Rachel remembered her reply, and it felt like a stone falling through the water to the bottom of a lake: "I can't stay. Not now. She needs me. She's going to send me to school, Jonathan, a really good school. I'm all alone now. She's my only family."

"You're not alone, Rachel," he had answered. "Don't you know that?"

What else had she said? The walls of the post office seemed to be closing in on her. She wished she were running on the prairie, running fast, throwing her arms wide, lifting her face to the wind. She wished she were breathing the prairie wind.

The stone hit bottom. She had left Beaver Creek for Vermont and she had gone to the college a half hour's drive from Grandma's house. And she had had it all, everything Grandma Budd had promised, the pretty room under the eaves, the nice friends, the wonderful teachers. She had had it all. A few weeks after arriving in Vermont, a letter had come from

Carl Linstrum saying that Jonathan had gone into the army, that he had gone to Vietnam, that he had gone to the war.

The letters from Carl Linstrum always brought news about Jonathan Walking Bear. Jonathan had returned from Vietnam but he was traveling around the country in some kind of trailer. Jonathan was somewhere in South America. Jonathan was working on a Navajo reservation in Arizona. And then, suddenly, Jonathan had come home. He was back in town.

He's changed, Linstrum had said. He was really wild sometimes. Drinking. Maybe he was on drugs, too; he wasn't sure. But something was wrong. She had taken the first plane back to Omaha, and then the Piper Cub for Silver City, and then the bus to Beaver Creek.

She remembered opening up the brick house on Sorrel, letting in the sun and the smell of freshly cut grass, and the peaceful hometown sounds. And she remembered waiting. Not doing anything, not unpacking her suitcase. Just waiting, through the silence of the afternoon.

It was past midnight when she heard the pickup truck. She went out on the porch to meet him. He stood at the bottom of the stairs looking up at her. He was wearing dirty jeans and a leather jacket. His hair was very short.

He looked like he was burning up inside. They had gone away together, driving out of the town in the dead of night, driving the hot flat roads day after day, from town to town, from motel to motel.

A month later she knew she had to get away from him. She went back to Vermont. In September she knew she was carrying his child.

Up on the bluff, the boy sat motionless. He had stopped looking at the horizon. He had closed his eyes and sat cross-legged, feeling the bare earth under his hands. And the intense heat all around him.

"Sometimes the earth speaks to me through the eagle woman," Jonathan had said. That was the day he had wept.

Joe waited with his hands on the earth. The sky was changing color, but he didn't notice. The sky had darkened into a sickly shade of green. Great clouds of dust had begun to obscure the horizon. Suddenly a giant funnel shape appeared out of the swirling mass. It began moving rapidly across the prairie, turning freakishly as it came. And with it came a roaring.

Rachel burst from the post office without locking the door and ran toward her car. The boy would be with Jonathan. That's where he had said he was going. They would be together now. There would be no danger. Jonathan would know what to do, where to go. She drove fast. The storm warnings were coming over the radio at five-minute intervals. She passed a man who was running frantically along the sidewalk shouting someone's name.

The wind began buffeting her car as if it were a toy. Hunched over the wheel, she kept driving as fast as she could.

She had lied to her son; she had invented a father for him. The father Grandma Budd had dreamed of. "Are you going to tell him his father is a drugged half-breed?" she had shouted.

To the right of her, a tree was ripped up like a stick and flung to the ground.

He had frightened her, from town to town, waking up screaming. And the dogged heavy drinking, the drugged sleep, the occasional returns to his old self.

I should have had the courage.

I should have had the courage.

The wind shrieked around her.

Jonathan was running over the prairie, running fast. The dog had disappeared somewhere behind him. He was close to the bluff now. Suddenly he saw the boy through the swirling dust, struggling to climb down the side, his hands grasping for a hold—grass, rock, anything.

"Joe!" he shouted, but the wind threw his

voice back in his face. He pushed himself forward and was thrown to the ground so violently he couldn't breathe for several seconds.

He began to crawl toward the dark mass of the bluff, obscured by the dark sky and the dust. It seemed hours before he reached the base. He started to climb toward the place where he thought he had seen the boy. His nails were like claws, gripping the earth, forging a hold where there was none. Pushing up with his feet, reaching, grasping, clawing, reaching again.

Then his fingers closed around a tennis shoe. "Joe!" he shouted.

The boy released his hold; they struggled down the incline together, half rolling, half falling.

"Dig!" Jonathan yelled, scraping at the earth with his knife and hands. Wildly they labored the flank of the bluff until they had hollowed out a small protection from the storm. Jonathan pushed the boy against the wall of earth and lay over him, trying to shelter him from the demented wind. They huddled there. Time had disappeared. There was only the screaming and the gritty taste of dirt in their mouths.

Then, as suddenly as it had come, the storm was gone.

Their faces were smeared with earth; they could feel it under their fingernails, in their clothes. They looked at each other in the copper-colored light.

"Why in God's name did you come out here?"

"I was : . . I wanted to have a vision, like you. To know something. I cleared out the space and I tried to speak to the directions like you said. Then the tornado came."

"It was one hell of a twister."

"How did you know I was out here?"

"You left a pretty clear trail for a hunter like me. Not to mention Trump."

They stopped talking.

Someone was calling their names. "Joe! Jonathan!"

They stood up and stepped away from their shelter under the bluff. Rachel was running toward them over the high grass. She was running lightly and fast. Her hair was flying wildly. As she saw them she shouted their names again. Trump was running in front of her, his tongue hanging out and his ears flying.

She stopped a few yards away. Her breath came in short gasps.

She looked first at Joe, then at Jonathan. "You're safe," she said.

"Looks that way, doesn't it?" said Jonathan.

Then she sank to the ground, like a scarf someone just dropped. "The house is gone," she said. "It's all ripped apart. Everything."

She began to cry softly. Trump waddled over and pushed his nose against her face. Lowering his head, he licked her hand.

Joe took a step back. Because Jonathan Walking Bear was lifting his mother to her feet. He saw their faces come together. The sky had turned very bright over them. Jonathan was holding his mother in his arms, rocking her like a child, murmuring to her. Their voices blended, rising and falling. He couldn't hear what they were saying. He took a few steps forward.

"We'll build a new house, Rachel. Out here facing the bluff."

Then Joe knew.

The ghost inside him faded.

Jonathan Walking Bear turned and opened his arms.

Joe ran straight into them.

1 8 6 0

The Tree

How long had she been alone? She no longer knew. The days all seemed the same. Maybe they didn't know Ben had died. Of course they didn't know. How could they? No one had come by. She had dug the grave alone. She had wrapped his body in her best good sheet and hauled it from their dark house in the hillside. She had rolled and pushed him over the edge of the hole it had taken her two days to dig. She had shoveled the heavy prairie earth back in. And then she had lain there, alongside the freshly turned earth, the same earth they had built the front wall with. She had stayed there till the stars came out and the moon was high, listening numbly to the familiar night sounds, a cricket, the swishing of the high prairie grass, a faraway coyote, then falling once again into the depths of her grief as if she were drowning. No one had come by.

Now she sat in the old rocker in front of the dugout, feeling the wide flat land stretching out all around her. She was trying to remember if she had eaten anything. Perhaps she had drunk some water from the pail. Through the darkness she could hear the light rustling of the apple tree she and Ben had planted. They had planted it right in front of the dugout, twenty steps from the doorway, so she could see it as she went about her chores. They had brought it with them from Missouri. She remembered how they had kept it alive during the long haul in the prairie schooner, dripping water over the clod of earth and roots. First thing, they had planted it. Before they even began work on the house.

What month was it? It had been August 10 the day Ben died. Now it was September. She had a calendar pegged up on the earth wall next to the fireplace. It was September for sure, but she didn't know what day exactly, because she had stopped tearing off the pages. Back there, during the time just after Ben died, she had lost count. Maybe it was the fourth or the sixth of September now. The earth over his grave had hardened. The nights were getting longer. She had felt bad about not having some

kind of cross for the grave, so she had broken
one of her blue porcelain plates, smashed it into
little pieces with the hammer, and formed the
letters of his name, pushing them into the earth
the way children do with a sand castle.

Why hadn't she left for Hoskins' farm? Why
hadn't she packed up a few things and gone to
Hoskins'? It was only a day's walk. With the
horse it would have been no more than four
hours, but there was no more horse. Just the
old wagon. And the harness hanging empty in
the shed. Still, she could have made the effort
to walk to Hoskins'. She could have taken some
cold corn bread and a jug of water tied up in
a cloth. But something held her there, day in
and day out. Was it Ben's grave? Was it because
she couldn't bear to leave him alone? Ben alone
in the ground? Was it because leaving him behind her, walking away from him, meant that
he was really dead?

Sometimes during the days she would pull
the old rocker out of the dugout and sit in it,
watching the shiny leaves fluttering in the
young apple tree, listening to their rustling. She
had taken good care of that tree. She and Ben
had planted it so carefully, tending it like a
baby, bringing water to it from the stream a
half mile away until they dug the well. It was
the only tree for miles around. She used to brag

about it to the other women when they met at the trading post. You'd have thought she was talking about a child, the way she carried on about the tree. How it had bloomed the first spring on the prairie. How the trembling young leaves gave off a special light in the late-afternoon sun. And how someday she would sit under it and how its wide branches would shelter her from the hot prairie sun.

Sometimes she had dreamed of herself sitting under the apple tree and in the dream she would always be making something for a child. Her belly would be round and she would be sewing something for a child.

But there had been no child after three years, and now Ben was dead. Yet she couldn't bring herself to leave the place. She couldn't walk away. Not even from the dugout that had made her weep the first time she saw it.

"You mean we're going to live in a hole in the ground?" she had cried.

"Just at first, honey," he had soothed her. "We'll have a real frame house by and by. Look, most of the work's already done. And the fellow who sold out said the place is real cool in the summertime and warm as toast in the winter."

She had helped him plow up the thick prairie sod to build the front wall. They had made the bricks together, chopping down on the long swaths of earth with a sharp spade, hauling them back to the dugout at the end of the day in the wagon. And together they had built the front wall, carefully piling the sod bricks up around the wooden frames for the door and the windows, filling the crevices between the bricks with loose dirt and mud.

She remembered the day they had pegged up the muslin from the four corners of the room to keep the bugs and snakes from falling down on them.

"It's like a tent, Ben," she had cried.

She was happy by then; she didn't mind anything anymore. She had hung brightly colored calico over the earthen walls and made a rag rug. She had started a quilt. That day she had thought she was pregnant. But the next morning she got her menses and she had said to Ben in a low voice that maybe she couldn't have children.

"Quit worrying yourself, Louisa," he had said. "Best way not to have children is to worry yourself."

And he had gone out to work in their fields. She could see him walking away from her for the day's work. She could see his slow, tall, kind movements as he walked away from her for the day's work.

The sun was sinking lower in the sky. Tonight, she thought, there would be just a little more darkness. Day after day, she knew the darkness was gaining ground. But for the moment the tree was still glimmering in the evening sun and she watched it. The pieces of china on Ben's grave were still shining brightly, catching the dying light. Suddenly a long shadow fell over her knees.

She looked up and drew in her breath all at once. A man was standing over her with his hat in his hands. He stood there quietly, a tall thin man with high cheekbones and rough red hands.

"Ma'am?" he said. "Excuse me, ma'am. I was wondering if you could spare a bite."

His voice was husky and low. He just stood there. He seemed to be wavering. She was looking up at his pale blue eyes, at his gauntness.

"Who are you?" Her voice came out in a whisper.

"Name's Shepherd, ma'am, Joshua Shepherd. Hoskins sent me out your way. Said you might be needing some help on the farm. I ain't had nothin' to eat for three days now, ma'am."

"Who are you?" she repeated, as if she had not heard him speak.

"Cowhand, ma'am. But I can farm."

Still she didn't seem to hear him.

"Are you all right, ma'am?"

The woman hadn't moved from the rocker.

She had turned her eyes away from the man and was looking at the tree again.

"Are you sick, ma'am?"

She heard herself answering him. "We've been through a bad drought. My husband died a few weeks back. Cholera. Caught it from some settlers passing through. I buried him myself over there by the tree."

The man said nothing. He bowed his head and kept on standing there by the rocker, turning his battered leather hat around and around in his long fingers.

Finally he said, "I'm real sorry to hear that, ma'am."

He kept on standing there over her, eyes on the ground, shuffling his boot-shod feet from time to time. The woman sat still as a statue, for she was floating far away, somewhere high over the endless flat land, moving numbly with the clouds, obedient to the winds.

Slowly the man became present to her and she saw his gauntness for the first time. He was thin and raw where Ben had been wide-shouldered, smooth-skinned. He looked frightened, as if he were a hunted animal of some kind. Whereas Ben, well, Ben was always the hunter. Couldn't be anything but. Nobody told Ben what to do. They maybe made suggestions, but Ben was the boss.

"I'm sorry," she said. "I'm not myself these

days. Please come into the house and have something to eat."

"Thank you kindly, ma'am," he murmured.

She got up from the rocker and walked back into the dugout. He followed her, bowing his head slightly to pass through the doorway. In the dimness of the earthen room, she felt for her mixing bowl in the cupboard. Quickly she lit a fire in the stove with some dried grass and buffalo chips and lifted her black skillet from its peg on the wall. She laid some bacon in the skillet, and while it fried, she made up the corn bread. The man sat at the table, still turning his old hat in his hands.

"Maybe you'd like to clean up some," she said. "There's a pump out back at the bottom of the hill."

He looked embarrassed. "I can't get up, ma'am," he mumbled. "My head's a-spinnin'. I hope I don't pass out on you."

She reached for the dipper in the pail of water by the door. "Here, here," she murmured. "I'm sorry to be so inhospitable. I'm not myself, you see."

The man put his hat on the table and, grasping the dipper with both hands, emptied it at once. She filled it again, and then a third time. He handed it back to her, whispering a thank you. But as she worked, he kept very quiet,

elbows resting on his knees, head bowed, eyes on the smooth, hardened earth floor.

"Bread's in the oven," she said. "I'll get you the bacon now."

She lifted the slabs from the skillet with her long fork, though they were not quite cooked through, and put them on a plate. The man ate with his fingers, burning them, chewing ravenously. When the corn bread was done, she cut him a big piece and put it on the plate and poured some molasses over it. She gave him a spoon, but he ate with his hands once again, holding the plate under his chin, breaking the dripping hot bread into his mouth, swallowing almost without chewing. She watched him, remained standing like a servant to one side of his chair. When he finished one helping of the bread, she gave him another, pouring the molasses over the yellow morsels as if for a child. He ate everything. At last she dipped a clean cloth in the pail of water and gave it to him to wipe his hands and face.

Night was coming on.

"Take the bed," she said. "You must be very tired. Lie down and get some sleep. Go right ahead. I don't sleep these days anyway."

"I couldn't do that, ma'am," he replied.

"Go on and lie down." She sounded as if she

were speaking to a child. "Just take those boots off first so you don't ruin my quilt."

Then the man complied silently.

She sat down on the floor in the doorway to the dugout, her back pressed up against the wooden jamb, and watched the last light disappear from the horizon. A small breeze was running through the leaves of her apple tree. She had saved it from the burning winds. Now the sound of the tree came to her like clear water running down a shallow brook. Behind her, in the darkness of the room, she knew the man was falling asleep. She could feel the fear leaving him like the deep current of an outgoing tide. Soon she knew that he slept. She knew also that his face was slowly changing. Without seeing, she knew that the thin lips were softening, that the high cheekbones were making peace with the rest of his face. And that the long, work-worn hands were loosening, until he lay on his back, palms open as if he were receiving as a gift the first stars in the great wide prairie sky.

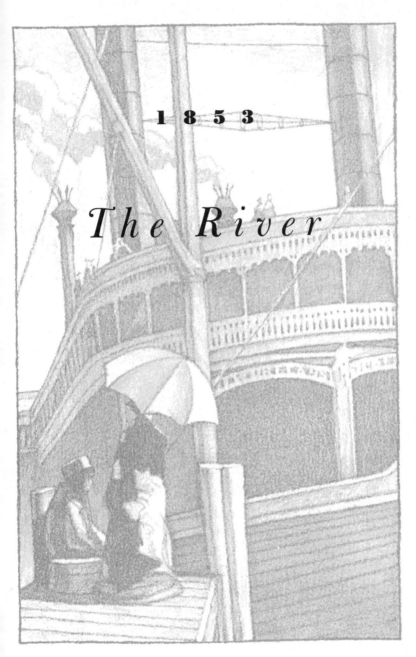

1 8 5 3

The River

When she boarded the steamer at Natchez, everybody could tell right away what kind she was. From group to group along the decks, the travelers' eyes turned to take in the look of her, the blond curls piled high, the jaunty set of her hat, the gossamer veil barely masking a bright red mouth. Senses suddenly alert, they listened for the swishing of her black-and-lavender silk dress as she passed by, and to the sharp thudding on the deck of her sleek little high-heeled boots. From group to group, passengers cast quick glances at the way she twirled her parasol at an angle and at the sassy movements of her hips, and just the smell of her perfume, heavy and sweet, set tongues to wagging from one end of the riverboat to the other.

Some of the women smirked as she passed, followed by a tall black slave bent under the weight of her trunk. They were farmers' wives in plain gingham dresses and drab bonnets, bound for the Kansas frontier, and their chattering became whispers in her wake.

As the steamer pulled slowly away from the dock, its great paddlewheels churning down into the muddy water, she entered the long, gilded saloon, still followed by her servant with the trunk on his back. Men looked up from their card games to watch her sashaying toward the plushly carpeted corridor at the far end of the enormous room. Some of them whistled, none too silently, between their teeth. And later on they would stare from time to time toward the shadows of the corridor, straining to see the closed door of the private stateroom into which she had disappeared.

After handing in the lady's trunk, her slave stayed right in front of the door, arms folded over his powerful chest, expressionless and unmoving. There was some talk about getting him down below where he belonged, but nothing came of it, and he kept to his post like a soldier.

At sundown, the woman not having emerged from her stateroom, the talk was mostly about her at the dinner tables over the fried chicken

and hot biscuits, particularly among the farmers' wives.

"Looks to me like that hussy don't want no truck with honest folk."

"Didn't you see? The niggra brought her everything on a tray."

"Well, I wouldn't set down at the same table with her if you paid me."

"Where do you suppose she's headed?"

"St. Louis, I'd guess."

"Some cathouse in St. Louis, you mean."

"I heard somebody say she was French, from New Orleans."

"Well, it's a crying shame that honest women like us have to sleep in cramped cabins while the likes of her can loll around in a stateroom."

"I seen her door. I walked by it. There's an oil painting on it. They all have one. All them stateroom doors. And you can smell that perfume of hers as you walk by. It just seeps out into the hall."

"Was the darky there?"

"He ain't budged. Stays by that door like a dog."

Later that evening, in the crowded saloon, the cigar smoke of the wealthier passengers hung heavy in the air under the tinkling chandeliers. A curly-haired man in a bowler hat, moving from table to table, had gained the attention of several card players and was pulling a swath of lithographs from a briefcase, showing them off and talking excitedly, his face pink with exertion.

"Look at the town hall, sir," he exclaimed. "Look at those shade trees! There's two churches. Why, it's even got an opera house! See for yourselves!"

The men began passing the lithographs from hand to hand.

"Now, I am the exclusive agent for this fine Kansas town," said the man in the bowler, pulling a chair up to the table. "And let me tell you gentlemen that I'm offering you the chance of a lifetime here. Fifty lots of fine fertile land is what I've got to offer! Sign up and you won't regret it, no, sir! This town has a big future and I'm sure you and your families will want to be part of it!"

An elderly merchant who had boarded in New Orleans chuckled softly from his deep leather armchair and leaned toward a younger traveling companion. Gesturing with his brandy snifter so that the golden liquid spun in the glass, he said, "See that fellow over there in the bowler jawing away about his Kansas town?"

"I've been watching him for a while, yes, sir," said the younger man.

"Well, that town of his, more than likely, ain't nothing more than a bunch of stakes in the ground out on the prairie. I've seen those boys operating before. Knew a man got took by 'em once; lost all his savings."

"Well, why don't you warn those poor folks over there?"

The older man chortled again. "Snakes like him have to live just like everybody else. Let him strike, I say. If those clodhoppers are too dumb to figure him out, too bad. He puts a lot of work into that routine. I almost admire him for it."

"You're an immoral sort of fellow, aren't you?"

"Live and let live, my boy. Eat or be eaten." He lifted his brandy glass. "And while we're at it, here's to the invisible lady down the hall there in her stateroom. May her fortunes prosper!"

The younger man lifted his own glass to his lips and they both drank slowly, allowing the sweet burning of the liquid to linger on their tongues.

In the last light of day, the steamer continued moving upriver, hugging the bank, keeping to the easy water, avoiding the powerful currents in the middle that would have slowed her northward progress. Along the banks on both sides of the great river, the trees bent low over the water, their leaves like lips against the cool stream, kissing their own dark shadows.

And in the carpeted hall the black man stubbornly kept watch before his mistress's door.

On the evening of the third day upstream, the wife of the elderly merchant from New Orleans, a stout lady in yellow satin, ventured to speak to the Negro, saying, "Look here, boy, is your mistress quite all right in there?"

"Madame don't wish to be disturbed," the tall slave answered. "And I am here to see that she ain't," he added in a louder voice.

"Well, I'm surprised the captain allows it" came the indignant reply. "You've got no business up here in the first place, talking back to white folks."

"I'm jest doin' what I has been told to do, ma'am," said the black man, bowing his head.

The woman stood there for a minute, staring openly at him. "I shall speak to the captain about you and that creature in there," she said in a tight voice. "Make no mistake about it!" She moved away with a soft snort, waddling back down the corridor toward the lights of the saloon.

From the depths of the riverboat, the boilers rumbled, then settled down to a low hum. And conversation in the long, gilded room shifted and turned like the river, lingering at some tables over the latest epidemic of yellow fever that had broken out in New Orleans. Some people were all for limewater as a safeguard against the deadly sickness, while others swore by garlic and onions. Or quinine. Or gin and sulphur. Or even firing cannon into the air.

A thick fog had begun to rise.

Inside the glass-encased house at the top of the steamer, the pilot listened for the calls of his leadsman sounding the depths: "Mark twain! Quarter twain! Mark three!"

Conversations slowly dwindled and died. Senses numbed by the fog, the travelers went to their beds.

Sleep came to most of the passengers more quickly than usual. And deep into the night, some men dreamed of lifting a gossamer veil to press their mouths against soft red lips, and some women of feeling silk on their bodies and of wearing heavy, sweet perfume and of having all men's eyes turn toward them as they passed.

The boat was moving very slowly now through the fog. No one saw the two figures emerge from the stateroom, walking swiftly and soundlessly down the gilded saloon and out onto the deck. The woman's blond curls caught the tiny drops from the fog right away. She was wearing nothing but a cotton shift.

"Solomon, are you sure we have to do this?" she whispered.

The tall man had a rope coiled over his shoulder. He walked straight to the railing, tied a double knot, and threw the rope over the side.

"I'm sure enough," he replied. "That woman kept looking at me all evening long, like she suspected something. And I saw her talking to the captain. We've come so far, we can't take any chances now."

He went first, stepping quickly over the railing, easing himself down the rope into the dark water. The woman seemed to hesitate for an instant, but a strong pull from the man below urged her to action, and grasping the rope with both hands, she, too, slid down toward the water, lowering herself gently to his side.

She slipped both her arms around his neck, and they stayed that way for an instant, treading water together. And then, with one dripping hand, he slid the blond wig from her head, revealing close-cut, curly dark hair.

"Don't you ever wear that perfume again," he whispered, kissing her lips, from which all trace of red had disappeared. "Now, swim!"

She let go of him and struck out for the riverbank. He followed, pushing through the water with long, sure strokes.

1 8 5 3

The blond wig floated for a time on the river. By the time it had sunk, settling softly on the muddy bottom, the man and his light-skinned wife were a good mile into Illinois, walking fast, tasting their first hour of freedom.

"The River" was inspired by true stories of black men and women who used disguise to escape from slavery in the Southern states. *The Liberty Line / The Legend of the Underground Railroad* by Larry Gara (University of Kentucky Press, 1961), pages 42–69.

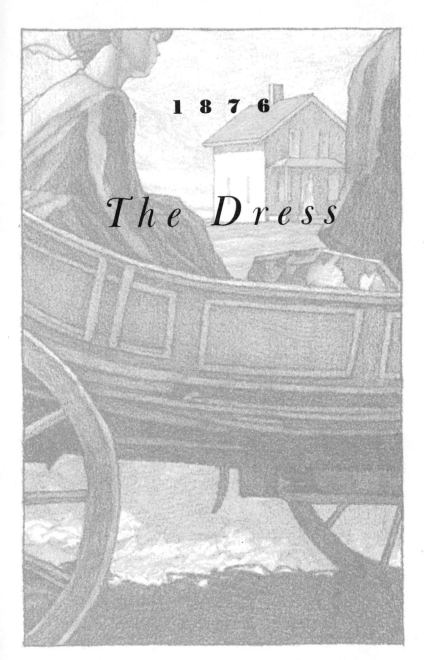

1 8 7 6

The Dress

"**I**'m not going," said the girl. "I'm not going out there to stay with that crazy old woman."

"You mind your manners, missy, and do as you're told. She's your aunt and she has agreed to take care of you while I'm gone."

The man rose from the table to give emphasis to his words, to stand over the dark-haired child just beginning to turn into a woman. He was the town blacksmith, swarthy and tall, with rumpled hair and large, powerful hands, and he felt helpless.

She sat there in her too-short cotton dress, looking straight ahead through tangled brown hair, sullenly kicking the table leg with one bare foot. The blacksmith noticed with a twinge the single, carelessly braided plait hanging down her back.

"There ain't nobody in town to look after you
while I'm gone this time," he began again in a
louder tone. "You know Mrs. Barton is sick in
bed with the ague. Now, you're going to stay
with your aunt and that's that."

The girl kicked the table leg again, hard
enough to make the dishes rattle.

"I'll be back from St. Louis in two weeks, and
that's a promise," he went on, more gently.
"Now, bear up, Laura. Aunt Ella won't hurt
you. You'd think she was an old witch, the way
you carry on."

"You said yourself she was crazy, touched in
the head. I heard you." The girl wasn't giving
up that easily.

"Well, you don't always say what you mean
when you're out of sorts. Your Aunt Ella's just
sad over the bad things that happened to her
a long time ago."

"What happened to her?"

"I'll tell you about that when you're grown.
For the moment, it's no concern of yours."

"She was an Indian lover!" The girl's voice
stabbed at him. "She lived with them. She was
a dirty savage! I know all about it. I heard you
talking." The child accused him, sullen and
defiant.

The man gave no answer.

"I'm scared of her, Pa. Don't make me go."

"Stop your nonsense," he snapped, losing patience. "Your Aunt Ella never hurt a living soul in all her born days. Get your things ready. I'm taking you out there this morning."

After a long silence, the girl said, "Do I have to wear shoes?"

Then the man knew he had won. He answered briskly, "Yes, you have to wear shoes, and you have to fix your hair, too. You're not going out there looking like a ragamuffin."

Ella Morgan's house was a good five miles out of town. It was a simple frame house and it had been built on top of a hill surrounded by the seemingly endless rolling land.

Wade Morgan drove his daughter out in their buckboard, casting a glance every now and then at her stubborn profile, at the arms folded tightly across her chest where the buds of breasts were beginning to show. The dress was too short and he knew it. She was growing out of everything and no mother to see to her. He would bring her a new dress from St. Louis. And some ribbons, too.

He tried to think of something to say, but the words that came out rang hollow. "You be nice to your Aunt Ellie, you hear me?"

It was all he could manage.

The woman was tall. She stood very still in front of her house, in front of the white porch, waiting for them to drive up.

Laura realized as they approached the motionless silhouette that her aunt must have seen them coming for quite a while, must have watched them crossing the gently rolling land from the little town to the north.

"Well, Ella, here she is!" Wade called out as he helped Laura down.

His voice sounded nervous to the girl. Laura stood in front of the buckboard, shifting uneasily in her tight-fitting button-up shoes, while her father reached under the seat for the small carpetbag containing her clothing.

"Hello, Aunt Ella," she murmured, without looking up.

"Hello, Laura" came a strangely quiet voice.

Laura looked up into frank blue-gray eyes, very much like her father's and somehow wholly different. She looked at the whitening blondness of her aunt's hair. It was thick and fastened into a simple bun at the nape of her neck. The woman's mouth was rather wide; she had a peaceful forehead. Suddenly Laura realized she was staring and lowered her gaze.

"Come on in, both of you. It has been a long time," said the woman.

She did not reach out to touch either the man or the child.

They followed her up onto the porch and into the house. Laura breathed in a smell of wood and herbs and roasting chicken.

As they walked into the large central room, the woman turned to her brother and said, "I'm glad to see you change your ways, Wade."

"Now, Ellie, don't get on your high horse, don't get riled."

Her father sounded jovial, but Laura could still feel his nervousness.

"I'm not riled, Wade. You and the child have always been welcome here, as you very well know."

She spoke slowly, deliberately. But the girl could hear a strange music hiding in her voice somewhere, an undercurrent barely perceptible through the shifting tones.

Suddenly Laura realized she was seeing her aunt up close for the first time in her life.

Aunt Ella Morgan, her father's older sister, the one they talked about in low tones, always stopping when she came into the room. Once she had overheard her father saying, "Let her be. We've done enough harm as it is."

That was when her uncles and Grandpa and Grandma had come from Salinas for her mother's funeral. There had been the smell of freshly cut flowers all through the house, and that was when her father had said, "Let her be."

Laura had been very young then, only six, but she remembered how Aunt Ella had sat at the back of the church, stiff and proud in a new black dress. She had left right after the service, hadn't stayed for the family gathering, had driven straight out of town in her wagon, whipping up the horse to a gallop.

Now Laura heard her aunt saying, "Stay and have something to eat, Wade. Everything's ready."

"I don't want to put you to any trouble, Ellie."

"It's no trouble. I'm happy to have you."

Laura looked around the room. It was square and light, with a fireplace at one end and a cast-iron stove at the other. Everything was spotlessly clean and the floorboards were tight and sanded smooth. A small blue door, slightly ajar, led to a spare room on the south side of the house. All the furniture was plain, except for a large, ornate chest of drawers standing between two windows facing west. Its dark, polished surfaces, the curling brass handles on the wide deep drawers, contrasted oddly with the stark simplicity of the room. Laura found herself staring again.

"It's pretty, isn't it?"

Laura looked up into the peaceful blue-gray eyes.

"Yes, ma'am," she answered politely.

"It belonged to my grandmother," said Aunt Ella, moving away from the girl and running her hand lightly over the smooth polished wood. "It was the one thing I wanted to keep when I came to live out here."

"You know you could have had anything you wanted, Ella," Wade said a little roughly.

"I didn't want anything else," she replied in a low voice.

The table was already set for three. They ate silently together, Wade seated at one end, Laura and her aunt facing each other. It was a good meal of roasted chicken, stewed squash, and hot white rolls with freshly churned butter, and an apple pie for dessert.

"You've put yourself out for us," said Wade after finishing a second helping of pie. "I haven't eaten like this since Christmas!"

Laura saw her aunt reach out and touch her brother's hand and in the same instant saw him recoil ever so slightly from her touch.

Aunt Ella folded her hands in her lap and said quietly, "You still can't bear it, can you, Wade?"

Wade rose from the table, like a swimmer rising for air. He patted Laura clumsily on the head.

"I'd better get going. I'll be back for Laura a week from Sunday. I'm mighty grateful to you. I'd better be going."

He seemed to stumble toward the door.

"Goodbye, Pa," said Laura in a small voice.

She remained sitting at the table with her aunt for several seconds as her father crossed the porch and walked out into the afternoon sun toward the buckboard. A tight knot had formed itself in the pit of her stomach; her hands had begun to perspire; she realized she was frightened.

"Perhaps we should go out and wave, what do you think?" said Aunt Ella.

Laura looked up. A tiny smile was playing at the corners of her aunt's mouth.

To her surprise, the knot in her stomach loosened its hold on her and the smile moved fleetingly over her own lips as well, as if they were sharing a secret.

"Yes, ma'am, let's do," she said.

They stood together on the porch and watched Wade drive away until he disappeared under the hill. They kept watching as he reappeared, as he gradually turned into a tiny dark spot moving north on the prairie.

"Now I'll show you where you're going to sleep," said Aunt Ella, walking swiftly back into the house. Her movements had become livelier, as if she were saying: Now we can breathe, now we can begin doing things. She led Laura through the blue door into a little room fitted out with a brass bed and a small cupboard. On top of the cupboard was an enamel washbasin with a large pewter pitcher standing in it.

"But this must be your room, Aunt Ella!" said Laura, suddenly realizing there were no other bedrooms in the house.

"I'll be sleeping in the main room while you're here."

"But where will you sleep? I didn't see any bed."

"Don't worry about me. I have a special bed. I'll show it to you later. Right now it's time for you to unpack. Where's that bag of yours?"

"Pa must have left it out on the porch."

"Well, run and fetch it!"

Together they put the girl's things into the cupboard, Laura lifting the neatly folded clothes from the bag, Aunt Ella laying them on the shelves. There wasn't much. Two sunbleached gingham dresses, a sunbonnet, two cotton petticoats, a nightgown, and underwear.

Aunt Ella closed the cupboard and said, "You can take those shoes off if you like."

Laura sat down on the bed at once and began undoing the buttons on the tight-fitting shoes. Aunt Ella, who had been kneeling in front of the cupboard, turned and helped her pull them off. Laura sighed and wiggled her toes.

Then, remembering her manners, she said, "Thank you, Aunt Ella, for having me."

The Dress

The woman didn't seem to hear her. She was looking down at the girl's bare feet as if in a dream. Laura felt the chill of fear return and run down her back.

But then the answer came in the strange melodious voice, "You are very welcome, Laura. I wish you had come sooner."

The words were out before she could stop them: "Pa wouldn't . . ."

"Wouldn't let you come?" Her aunt finished the sentence for her.

Laura flushed and began twisting a corner of her dress between her fingers. A long silence fell between them which the woman did not attempt to interrupt.

At last, Laura began to speak haltingly. "Sometimes I see you driving through town. Sometimes I see you from our front window. But you never stop. Sometimes I see you at the general store, too. Once, right after my mother died, I saw you there and I started to run across the street, but Pa came and grabbed me. And after that . . ." The girl's voice trailed off.

"And after that he told you I was crazy, touched in the head. A crazy woman living alone out on the prairie, year in and year out, these past ten years."

"Well, he never said it outright. But I've heard him talking with folks."

"With your neighbor, Liza Barton, for instance?"

"She's one."

"And old Pete Hansen, at the hotel?"

"How do you know them?"

"I know everybody who lives in that town of yours, child. That's why I stay out here."

"I don't understand."

"I live out here by myself because I have to."

"I still don't understand you, Aunt Ella."

The woman seemed to be dreaming again. She was still kneeling on the floor. At last, she said, "It's because I can't bear life any other way."

The girl didn't want her aunt to drift off again. Quickly, she asked, "Did they do something bad to you, Aunt Ella, all the people in town?"

"They did what they thought was right. They didn't understand it was the worst bad thing they could have done. That it was a crime like killing someone."

"But what did they do?"

The woman rose without answering. She extended a hand. "Come, I'll show you the rest of the place now."

Laura followed her aunt out of the house. It was hot, with a wind blowing from the south. All around them, the land spread out like an ocean. "Your hill is like a ship, Aunt Ella," she said. "I feel like we're in a big ship sailing on the sea!"

"Do you, now?" exclaimed her aunt. "That's the way I feel sometimes myself."

They crossed the rise toward a small stable and entered its warm shadows. From the depths of the stable came the sound of a horse shifting heavily in a stall, whinnying a welcome. Laura ran forward, lifting eager hands over the wooden barrier, touching a velvety nose, delighting in the great liquid eyes.

"Here," said Ella, handing her niece a bunch of hay.

The girl offered the hay at once, feeling the pull from the great soft lips, listening with a shivery pleasure to the crunching of the beast's strong teeth.

"Can I take care of him while I'm here? Can I brush and water him?" she asked.

"Of course, if you like. There's plenty of work to be done. You can feed the chickens, too, and fetch water and help me with the garden."

"Where's your garden, Aunt Ella?"

"Do you want to see it now?"

They began walking down the south side of the hill. At the bottom Laura could see a well with a shiny pump next to a small field with neat rows of corn and vegetables.

"Let's run!" said Aunt Ella suddenly. "I'll beat you to the well!"

And before the girl could get over her surprise, the woman had darted from her side and was halfway down the hill, her dress flying, her apron strings loose to the wind. With a cry, Laura was off behind her. At the bottom of the hill, Aunt Ella turned, panting, one hand on the pump handle, to watch her niece catch up.

"I won!" laughed Aunt Ella.

"You cheated!" cried Laura.

"Sure I did!" answered the older woman, placing her hands on her hips. Her hair had come undone and she suddenly looked years younger.

They walked between the rows of corn and beans and squash.

"It's a beautiful garden, Aunt Ella."

"It keeps me busy. And I can sell the extra produce in town. They don't mind that," she added with a chuckle. "They buy my vegetables, and my preserves, too. Do you know how to do preserves?"

"Well, sometimes I watch Mrs. Barton."

"Maybe I'll teach you while you're here."

The girl looked out toward the horizon. The question lying heavy in the pit of her stomach tormented her. She had to get rid of the weight.

"Aunt Ella, is it true that you were a savage with the wild Indians?"

The Dress

The woman turned toward the girl, moving as if she had been slapped. Her blue-gray eyes were cold. Laura hardly recognized her. The wind lifted the thick, loosened hair from her shoulders; her face was a storm. Then she wheeled away. Her body bent forward.

"That's none of your business," she whispered. She could have been choking.

"I'm sorry. I didn't mean to be rude." The girl was frightened now.

"Everyone's sorry. Everyone's so very, very sorry."

The woman righted herself and walked away from the girl without looking back. She walked straight out onto the prairie, her dress blowing around her legs. Laura watched her disappear behind a rise.

Laura went back to the house. She sat down at the table and looked around the room, studying the surface of the black cooking stove, the neat pile of kindling lying in a flat basket on the floor beside it. She contemplated the plain high cupboard where Aunt Ella kept her dishes and pans and cutlery. She walked over and opened one of the drawers and looked at the knives and forks. She touched the sharp tips of a fork and closed the drawer. Then she slid her hands into the smooth tin washbasin on the stove, lifted the heavy kettle for boiling water. There was still some water in it. Maybe she ought to go down to the well and get more. She sat down again and directed her gaze at the ornate chest of drawers standing between the windows facing west. Something dark attracted her eye in the corner to the right of the smooth and polished piece of furniture. It was a large, leathery bundle; it looked like some sort of animal skin. She decided she had better not touch it.

Spying a hickory broom next to the cupboard, Laura began to sweep the smooth wooden floor. It didn't really need sweeping, but she worked mechanically at her task, pushing the imaginary dirt out onto the porch and from the porch over the steps to the ground. She kept on sweeping for a long time, just to be moving and not frightened.

It was late afternoon when suddenly Aunt Ella appeared in the doorway. Her hair was entirely loose and streaming down her back, but her face seemed composed once more. Laura rose from the chair she had been sitting in.

Her aunt came forward and stood silently in front of her. "Forgive me, Laura. I hope I didn't frighten you."

"It's all right. I didn't mean to pry. Really I didn't. I won't ever ask you again. I promise."

The woman sat down at the table. Through

the western windows the sky was blazing red with sundown.

She folded her hands in her lap and began to speak slowly, pausing between her sentences.

"I was a young girl when they captured me. They took me at the stream where I fetched water every day. Your father was just a baby then . . .

"They tied me to a horse and took me to their village. I was a prisoner. I tried to escape several times, but they always found me and took me back. The last time I tried to escape, I was beaten to make sure I wouldn't try to run off again. Then they moved to their winter camp. It was many miles away and I no longer knew where I was. After quite a long time, I lost hope of ever seeing my family again.

"And then I married."

The girl did not speak, did not move. She stood in the reddening, darkening room, and her aunt's words continued to sound, the accent she had first sensed in the woman's speech becoming stronger and stronger.

"I married a Cheyenne warrior. He was kind to me. I no longer had to work hard. When he returned to the camp, my only task was to tether his horse for him. Each time he returned, he brought me gifts. And as time went on, I began to think much of him for his kindness to me. I began to look forward to the sound of his step and to the sight of his face.

"We lived together seven years. I spoke the Cheyenne tongue. I was the mother of his children. Two daughters and a son.

"Then, one day, the soldiers came and attacked our village. They came with their big guns. We were wiped out. I lost all. Husband and children. All. A blue-coat was about to kill me when he saw I was white. And so I was spared. And taken back to my family.

"They opened their arms to me, but in their hearts they were ashamed. In their hearts they despised me for what I had been. They locked me away, kept me hidden, so people couldn't look and point. Finally, when they were sure I wouldn't try to run back to the Cheyenne, they let me come live out here. It was my wish to be here, away from the town. Your father dug the well and built this house. He was happy, they were all happy to have me out of the way. Out of their midst. And so I have lived since that time."

Night had fallen and the room was dark. A silence descended over them like a heavy cloud. Ella rose without looking at the girl and went to the bundle in the corner of the room. She pulled it forward and opened it, a thick buffalo robe. Kneeling on the fur, she said, "This is my bed. Go to sleep now, Laura."

The Dress

The girl walked silently into the spare room. Soundlessly, she undressed, pulled her night-gown from the shelf in the cupboard, and slipped it over her head. Then she crept between the sheets and pulled the blanket up around her shoulders. In spite of the warmth, she was trembling.

Deep into the night, a sound awakened her, a low sound of sliding wood. She sat up in bed; the sound became more distinct. Laura got out of bed and took two steps forward. She looked through the half-open door into the darkness of the larger room. Slowly her eyes adjusted to the starlit gloom. Her aunt was kneeling on the buffalo robe in front of the shining chest of drawers, taking something from the bottom drawer. The thing was white and soft, Laura saw, yet there was a strange heaviness to it. Her aunt pressed the soft whiteness to her breast, then buried her face in it, seeming to breathe deeply, to breathe in this thing, taking it into her body as if it were giving her strength. From time to time, the white thing made tiny clicking sounds.

Then suddenly from the kneeling woman came a faint moaning. She had begun to rock back and forth, holding the white thing to her breast and belly and making the moaning sound. It was a sound like the wind, or like an animal crying in the wind, and then, fleetingly, it was like a song. But slowly it became entirely a song of a kind Laura had never heard before.

Then the woman rose, allowing the white thing to fall open, holding it in front of her, arms extended, and the girl saw it was a dress made of deer skins, very white, and she could see by the faint starlight coming through the window the shimmering of the shells with which it was decorated.

Aunt Ella stayed there quite a long time, holding the dress in front of her. And then she knelt and laid it carefully back in the wide deep drawer. She closed the drawer and lay down on the buffalo robe, pulled its great folds around her, and did not move again.

Laura crept back to her bed. Soon she could tell that the woman was sleeping in her buffalo robe on the smooth wooden floor. And she knew that the song had brought peace to her aunt. For a very long time, Laura listened to the woman's steady breathing, remembering the song, over and over, until a last wave of sleep carried her into unconsciousness as well.

1 9 0 4

The Train

The boy woke up with his face to the window and saw the moon setting in a pale sky. Something flickered in his mind. An unusual thing was going to happen today; they had told him about it; they were taking him somewhere. It was to be interesting. He tried to think what it was, but the memory wouldn't come. Sometimes his brain played tricks on him like this.

It was already hot; he could feel his nightshirt sticking to his back. He began stirring, then forced his head with a jerk toward the door. It was closed. He would have to wait for his mother to come. He would have to wait for her to raise him and dress him and then to call for his father, who would carry him downstairs, down to the new rattan wicker chair with wheels. They had sent off for it to Chicago from a picture in the Sears and Roebuck catalogue for 21 dollars and 75 cents. It had been the most expensive of the three invalid's chairs shown on the page, but his mother had insisted. "He'll be more comfortable in it," she had said. "It's made to go outdoors, and there are hand rims attached to the wheels." The chair had come three weeks later to the train station, and Pa had driven over with the wagon to fetch it.

"Well, Tom," his father had said jovially after he put him in the chair for the first time. "You'll be able to get around a little on your own now if you can manage to push those newfangled wheels."

"He'll learn," his mother had answered quickly.

He recalled how his excited spasmodic hands had first squeezed ineffectually at the round metallic rims. But after a day or so, he was able to make the chair go all the way across the front porch. When he got to one end, Ma or Pa or Emily would turn him around and he would push himself to the other end. They had all clapped and Pa had said, "Good for you, Tom," in a big voice.

His thoughts turned back to the coming day. He tried again to remember what was going to happen. Suddenly, he was sure it had something to do with the train station. That was it: someone or something on the train.

The Train

He heard the rooster crowing and then the dog began barking, fast and excited. He wished his mother would come, but the house was still very quiet. He forced his head back toward the window. The moon had become transparent, disappearing into the blue. They had put his bed next to the window now that summer had come, so he could look out and have a little breeze. But there was no cool air yet this morning. His forehead had begun to feel clammy. Why didn't she come? Suddenly, muffled clattering sounds began to rise from the kitchen, and he knew with a twinge of relief that she was getting breakfast ready.

He pushed the sheet down to his waist, feeling his face cringe with the effort. People didn't like looking at his face, the way it got twisted every time he tried to move. They didn't like the sounds he made when he tried to speak. He could tell from the way they turned away, trying to seem natural. From the way they kept on talking in bright tones, as if he weren't there.

Then, all at once, his mother was with him. The door had opened so gently he had not heard. Leaning over him in her dressing gown, she felt cool, smelling of lavender, her dark hair still down around her shoulders. She kissed his damp forehead and pulled the sheet all the way back and lifted him to a sitting position. He tried to say her name, but the word came out in a high-pitched groan. She slid the chamber pot from his bedside table, lifted his nightshirt, and, holding him expertly under the arms, allowed him to relieve himself. Now his nightshirt lay on the bed beside him and he listened to her pouring water from the big porcelain pitcher into the washbowl on the chest of drawers and then the cool damp cloth was on his back, along his arms and chest. He made no effort to move, waiting for the sound of water dripping back into the washbowl as she wrung out the cloth. He liked that sound. Repeatedly she returned with the coolness, washing his body swiftly and gently, then drying him with a big white towel, then getting him into his clothes, the way she did every day.

And then, just like every day, she called, "Aaron! Tom's ready for you!"

A tall, bearded man came in without speaking. His big hands slipped around the boy's back and under his legs, lifting him easily and carrying him out of the room. His head resting against the man's wide shoulder, Tom listened to the familiar soft steps on the carpeted floor of the hall, then to the sharper, steady thumping down the polished wooden stairs. He breathed in his father's smell of pipe tobacco and soap; he liked the going down in the morning. Wings, he thought, as they descended together. Wings like a bird. He could see the gray wicker chair waiting at the bottom of the steps, the dark rubber wheels, the wonderful, shiny hand rims.

What was it that was going to happen? Again he fought to remember as his father lowered him into the chair and the smell of coffee drifted around them. He could see his mother on the landing above him, leaning over the banister, brushing out her hair. He could see her because his head was still thrown back and he hadn't yet tried to grip the wheels. "Emily!" she was calling as she worked on a thick strand of hair. "Go get the biscuits out of the oven."

A little girl ran in from the front porch, leaving the door open behind her. "Can I push Tom's chair?" she called out.

The morning sun poured into the front hall, engulfing the boy in light.

"Get the biscuits out first," said the man. "Then you can push Tom out on the porch."

She ran past him, a flash of blue dress and light hair. His hair was dark, like his mother's. But she was blond like Aaron. And one day she would be tall.

There was some hurried rattling from the kitchen and she returned, eagerly grasping the back of the chair. The wicker made little ticking sounds as she pushed and guided the chair toward the front door, bumping it over the door jamb. She rolled him across the porch up to his place at the table already neatly set for four. The place where he always sat, to the right of his mother. Wings, he thought again, the image coming to him without reason. Wings like a bird. Wings for floating over the house and the farm. He imagined the soaring. Like the crows he could see from his window hovering over his father's cornfields. Like the hawk he had seen the other day, just for a few seconds, floating, almost motionless, high in the air, then plunging straight down and rising with a small prey in its claws. He lost himself in the rising.

A spoon was coming toward his mouth. "Oatmeal, Tommy," she was saying.

And at the same instant he heard his father's voice in the middle of a sentence. "Yes, sir, the old buzzard was something all right . . ."

Opening his mouth, closing his lips around the sweet porridge, swallowing carefully, he directed his gaze across the table at the big man spreading butter on a biscuit.

"Yes, sir, he had a quarter of the United States Army running after him in those mountains, after him and less than twenty other braves."

The answer was coming. He made a sound. It came out low, then dying away. They pretended not to hear.

"Lots of folks are going over to the station to see him."

Someone was coming on the train. Someone on the train.

"Mean as a snake, though," his father went on. "Cruel. Slit more white throats than I care to think about."

"Is he dangerous?" asked Emily with a thrill in her voice.

"Lord, no! He's an old man now, honey. Nobody knows exactly how old. He was a holy terror, though, back in the 1880s when he was giving the army a run for their money. I saw him myself in my soldiering days, back in '86, when he surrendered to General Miles in Skeleton Canyon."

There was a short silence and then he added, "I've got to admit I'm right curious to have another look at him."

"Perhaps I'll stay home," said the woman quietly.

"Nonsense, Lily!" exclaimed the man.

"Ma!" cried the little girl at the same time. "Don't you want to see him?"

"Oh, I guess so. But I don't feel right about it somehow. He's a prisoner over there at Fort

Sill. They ought not to parade him around like that. Like some animal in a zoo."

"You'll let me go, won't you, Pa?" Emily's voice was coaxing, the pretty child already knowing she would get her way.

"We're all going," said the man with authority. "Your ma, Tom, all of us."

"If you say so, Aaron," answered the woman. "But I still say there's something immoral about it."

He leaned over and whispered to her, "Oh, hush up, Lily, you're ruining everything. I'm going out back to fetch the wagon."

The old man was dreaming. He sat in the rattling passenger car, his head against the window, his eyes closed, his limbs relaxed. The train rocked him and he dreamed on. He saw the four masked dancers coming out among the people. Some women ran toward them, reaching out to them for strength, reaching out to the mountain spirits these men had become, for the healing powers that were theirs to give today.

The great steam engine pulled the train along the rails across the flat land, but the old man was far away, high in his mountains, his camp near a good stream. A young girl had recently come of age and the masked dancers

were moving among the people, giving sacred
power and health. All things were as they
should be.

He woke up. It had been a good dream. He
felt strengthened. He could look out at the flat
land of Oklahoma running by and think about
the day before him. He placed one hand on a
rectangular wooden box on the seat beside him.
He lifted the box and rattled it gently. Small
clicking sounds came from the inside. A slight
smile softened his severe features. He leaned
his head back against the window, listening to
the steady pumping of the steam engine and
the rhythmic rumbling of the cars on the tracks.
He closed his eyes but did not sleep. Soon they
would be stopping. Soon he would hear the
wheels beginning to scrape; soon he would feel
the jarring, the gripping of the brakes.

The train had come to a complete halt in
front of the station for several minutes when
the old man emerged from the passenger car.
Stepping carefully down onto the platform, he
walked toward a small crowd of people gath-
ered at one end. At the sight of him, a kind of
sigh arose from the group and they began shifting and murmuring among themselves, staring
at the old man as he approached. He was wearing white man's clothes, a faded blue army
jacket with a long row of buttons, trousers of

the same hue, and cowboy boots. The boots were very shiny, as if he took good care of them. But his rather untidy gray hair was almost shoulder-length, and he wore the traditional wide Apache headband.

With a glance, the old man took in their hungry, curious eyes, noticing at once in some of them the tiny flicker of fear, and he adjusted his walk ever so slightly toward a shuffle.

They began jostling now he was almost among them, people at the back craning their necks for a better look.

The high-pitched voices of children reached the old man's ears. "Can I see?"

"Pick me up, Pa!"

And then the old Apache was surrounded.

Some hands reached out furtively to touch his sleeve, then more boldly, pressing for a feel of the arm beneath the cloth. They were all around him, some pushing their children forward.

"Hey, Geronimo!" a man shouted from the back of the crowd. "Could you do a war whoop for us?"

There was some nervous laughter.

Then somebody else yelled, "How about a little war dance, Geronimo?"

A sun-bleached bench stood against the clapboard wall of the station. The old man sat down on it and reached deep into the pocket of his trousers. The people drew back a little.

Ponderously, he pulled out an army jack-knife. They watched him open it, noticing his strong, agile, and surprisingly small hands. The blade glittered briefly in the late-morning sunlight and the people in the crowd felt a sudden thrill piercing at their throats, then digging at their bowels. They watched. The old man was cutting a button off his coat, slowly and carefully slitting the threads which attached it to the material. He held out the small round piece of metal in the palm of his hand.

"Button," he said. "You want to buy it?"

Somebody called out, "How much?"

"Five cents," said the old man. "One button from Geronimo's coat, five cents."

The people crowded in again.

"I'll take it!" cried a woman. "Here's my five cents."

"Would you cut off another one?" someone shouted.

"Can I have one, Pa?" called a child.

"Buy another button?" asked the old man.

"I'll take one! Me, too! Here's a nickel! Here's mine!"

The voices mingled, faster and faster.

Someone was pushing an invalid's chair forward from the back of the crowd. A man's voice rang out, "Here, folks, let my boy see, would you please?"

Somebody yelled, "Let Aaron's child through, everybody!"

The old man looked up from his work. He had just cut the last button off his coat.

A twisted boy child, his knees pressed together, his head thrown sideways, his hands hooked inward, was sitting before him in a chair with wheels. A tall, bearded man stood behind the chair; at his side a small, dark-haired woman was holding a little girl in her arms.

The bearded man smiled awkwardly. "One for us, too, please," he said, holding out his coin.

The old man had stopped moving. He seemed to have gone somewhere else. He was looking at the boy, but he was gone. A strange silence fell upon the crowd. And then he was taking hold of the child's hand. The old man could see the boy's eyes were fixed on him, large dark eyes looking up at him as from the bottom of a well. Slowly, the aged Apache forced the small clenched fingers open and pressed the button into the palm, closing the fingers back over it. Still holding the child's fist, he leaned forward and whispered something to him. Then he rose, closed the jackknife, put it back in his pocket, and walked down the platform without another word toward the passenger car from which he had emerged. His boots made a thudding sound on the warm planks.

Tom felt the button in his hand. His heart was beating fast. He tasted dust on his tongue from the long ride over between the cornfields. He watched the old man climb back up into the train. A few soldiers who had been loitering in front of the passenger car climbed back in after him.

Then came the jangle of the engine bell, the enormous sigh of the steam, and the train pulled slowly out of the station, carrying the old man away.

"What did he say to you, Tom?" asked his father in an excited voice as he wheeled his son back toward the wagon. "He said something, didn't he?"

Tom did not attempt to speak. He had not understood the old man's words. But for an instant they had sounded like wings, like wings in the wind. He let them keep sounding through his mind, again and again. He held the button tightly in his hand.

Back in the rumbling train, the old man had returned to his seat.

"Good business today, old fellow, eh what?" said one of the soldiers from the other end of the car with a laugh.

The Train

The old man did not answer. He opened the wooden box on the seat beside him. There were two compartments in it. One held coins, the other a supply of buttons. He took off his coat. Digging down among the buttons, he pulled out a needle and thread. Placing the coat on his lap, he selected a button from the box and began sewing it onto the coat. He had plenty of time before the next station and he did his work carefully and well.

1992

A Box

of Pictures

The square white box slips from my hands and topples onto the floor, spilling its contents with a dry splash. Damn! Why hadn't I taped the top down? Falling to my knees, I gather the scattered images together impatiently—Polaroids, snapshots, clippings, postcards—slapping them back into their shiny white cardboard container as fast as I can. I will have to sort all this out sometime, but the box is almost full, a heaving little sea of images. A terrible job. So many pictures that never got pasted into an album, never even labeled or dated. I am bad at labeling and dating. Perhaps, because it always makes me think of death. I sigh, sit down on the floor cross-legged, and begin going through the unruly pile.

———

Here is a summer picture. On the Mediterranean, on the coast of Catalunya, the headland at Cap de Creus where the wind never ceases, where the ground is strewn with dark and shiny flat mica stones, high up by the lighthouse, overlooking the sea. My three children are standing up against the white wall of the lighthouse, smiling and waving in their light summer clothes.

A black-and-white snapshot. My parents' little vacation house near the ocean at Gause Landing in North Carolina, all dappled with shadows from the overhanging Spanish moss spilling down in gossamer strands from a huge live oak. Eighteen years ago, I huddled there together with my father and my brother and my two sisters as my mother lay dying in a hospital a half hour away. An elderly black woman sat behind me, old Emma, who took care of my mother all through the bad last days. She sat behind me, braiding and unbraiding little strands in my hair. I was living in France by then; I was married with children by then; but the old woman played tirelessly with my hair in a soothing manner as if I had been a child.

Front porch. For a second I wonder where. The porch swing is hanging empty. Someone has just gotten up and gone into the house. The picture is blurry, the hanging bench was still moving when the photograph was taken. Probably my work on a trip back to the States from France, grabbing hungrily for an American icon. I decide it is my brother's house in Washington, D.C., where he lived right after he got married.

A dark, shiny print, taken with a telephoto lens. Two angels in Venice, painted by Tintoretto, transparent in shadow—you can see right through them—high on a wall of the Scuola San Rocco.

A whole batch of Venice postcards. Tintoretto, Giorgione's *The Tempest*, Tintoretto, Tintoretto, Tintoretto.

Vacation picture, North Carolina. Pale colors, overexposed: the shadows of birds flying low along a wide beach.

My husband, our three children, and I. Standing with old Emma in front of her poor wooden house, practically a shack, on a back road behind the ocean, many years after my mother's death. I can't see my youngest sister, who was with us that summer. She probably took the picture. Emma said to us that time in her raspy, vibrant voice, "I was born down at one end of this road, I lived most of my life up at the other end, and I guess I'm going to die right here in the middle."

Her grave is covered with seashells, but she never went to the beach.

A picture I took from the Pont de l'Alma. A barge piled high with sand moves up the Seine in the dying light.

Under it, stuck to it, there is a plain white card. I pull them apart. There are two lines printed on the card, one of many sent to us by an artist friend in New York, always with the same two lines:

WE ARE SHIPS AT SEA

NOT DUCKS ON A POND

Our house in Taipei when I was fifteen. There was a wall all around it. The top of the wall was studded with broken glass. Dad was press attaché at the embassy. It was so hot I remember running down the tatami-carpeted hall to my bedroom, throwing my schoolbooks on the bed, and pushing my face up against the air-conditioner. Out back in the courtyard behind the kitchen, the amah squatted and fanned the coals in her earthenware-pot stove. I could count to ten in Chinese, but I went to school in the American ghetto.

Taken from a train with my old Instamatic. From a train running south, the gray-green meandering of the Loire, the gently wandering waters of the Loire.

A Polaroid from a trip to New York last year. The immigrants' luggage piled high across the enormous echoing entrance hall of the museum at Ellis Island, the first display you see as you enter the museum. Their trunks, their battered suitcases, their boxes and blankets, all lying together in the great long pile. And standing there, I knew suddenly with absolute certitude that I could never go home again.

This is a bedroom in America. It is a small black-and-white photograph with serrated edges, the way they printed them back in the fifties. Where was this? Perhaps the house in Charlotte before my mother redid it. The room is bare except for a brass bed and a mattress in the corner between two windows. The kind of window you push up to open. The striped mattress has little hillocks and tufted hollows all over it. Light from the curtainless window falls across the bed in a wide swath. The translucent paper blinds are pulled halfway down. A light fixture hangs from the ceiling, two creamy glass bowls, one under the other.

Digging down, I pull out a postcard reproduction of a Walker Evans. As always with his photographs, I look at it for a while. The high-ceilinged morning room of a great Southern plantation house, so empty and so full of light and sweet decay.

Here is a white envelope, the kind that sticks shut automatically. You buy them in cellophane packets of a hundred in French supermarkets. But the glue on this envelope has long dried up. It won't stick shut anymore. Inside, I discover a very old postcard printed on cheap thin paper in blacks and browns. It is a photograph of the Alexanderplatz in Berlin, shortly after the war. The view of the square is framed by the dark jagged sidings of two broken windows. The picture was taken from high up, probably from the sixth or seventh floor of some gutted building. The street is lined with great piles of rubble; all the buildings are bombed-out skeletons. Yet people are walking down there and a tram is turning the corner. In the foreground, on the windowsill, there are scattered bits of glass

and plaster. My father must have picked it up in '48 or '49 when we were living there.

In the envelope there is also a blurry black-and-white snapshot. I am sitting on an elderly woman's lap on a wooden bench in our garden in Berlin. I am about five years old. The woman is my nurse, a German baroness reduced to poverty by the war. I remember learning to sing the "Lorelei" with her, up in the little room where she lived on the top floor of our house.

> *Ich weiss nicht was soll es bedeuten*
> *Dass ich so traurig bin,*
> *Ein märchen aus uralten zeiten*
> *Das geht mir nicht aus dem Sinn . . .*

She was a small, spare woman with strong hands and tanned skin, not too proud to wear a white apron and work for the Americans, not too proud to feed and bathe their children and teach them her language, to kiss them and smile at them with her keen blue eyes.

I pick up another postcard, one I bought in Amsterdam last year at the Anne Frank House. It shows the bookcase which once masked the entrance to the apartment where the family was hidden from the Nazis all those years. There are no books on its shelves. The bookcase is always swung open now, giving tourists access to the empty rooms, letting them see the place on the wall where Otto Frank measured his children's growth until they were all betrayed and discovered and taken away.

Here I am with my grandfather in Charlotte, a small color photograph. We are sitting on a sofa looking at a picture book together. I am nine years old; I have just recently returned from Germany with my parents. I remember one Sunday morning in our big house. My grandfather is still in bed, in his high four-poster mahogany bed. He has icy-blue eyes. I have climbed up on the bed for a snuggle. Grandpa is a terrible tease, but he is speaking seriously now because I have just said something he doesn't like. He gestures emphatically with his partially crippled hand and says, "There has got to be a dominant race." All at once, my stomach is tied in knots. I know in a rush that I am going to become a stranger to my grandfather.

A picture torn from a book. A sad-eyed but smiling woman on the Kansas plains, holding up the handles of a wheelbarrow filled with prairie sod. The year is 1890. She is looking at the camera.

A Bellini angel, all golden light. Venice again, a musician angel playing a mandolin, bent forward from the waist, head inclined, with a grave little smile, one foot up on a stone step, supporting the mandolin on his chubby knee. Venice again, and the time we arrived there late one December night, walking through heavy fog from the ugly parking-lot square, carrying our light luggage, walking through the fog, and then like a curtain lifting, emerging onto a canal.

A picture I cut out of a book with scissors. It was taken the same year as the Kansas woman. Chief Big Foot lying dead in the snow at Wounded Knee, a cloth wrapped around his head as if he had a toothache, his arms thrust grotesquely upward from the elbows, Big Foot dead among the massacred dead.

Here we are, lounging in the grass at the Fête de l'Humanité at La Courneuve, near Paris somewhere, in the dizzy seventies. My husband has our oldest daughter on his shoulders. She must be about six. I am sitting in the grass with the younger one. We all look like hippies. Our son is not yet born. The Chileans sang, *"El pueblo unido jamas será vencido."* We shouted until we were hoarse.

A white card whose edges are slightly yellowed, with my handwriting on it. I had copied down a Navajo text: "The horse's feet are mirage, his gait rainbow; sun strings his bridle, black rain his tail, cloud with little rain his mane; his ears are of distant lightning, his eyes big star twinkling, his teeth of white shell, his voice of black flute, his lips of large bead, his face of vegetation, his belly of dawn."

A folded piece of paper. I open it. A photocopy of a photograph of Geronimo. I kept it on my desk while I was working on his biography. He is leaning up against a sunlit wall, his arms folded over his chest. He has just surrendered. He has also just exchanged his high-topped Apache moccasins for a pair of Mexican leather boots with pointed toes. They are going to ship him to Florida in a boxcar. He would never see his mountains again.

Postcard. Probably from the Urubamba Gallery near Notre Dame, in Paris, one of my haunts. A Cheyenne woman's dress of white deerskin spread out flat on a pale blue background, the better to display the delicately colored designs on it. This makes it look as dead as Chief Big Foot.

My husband, our daughters, and me carrying our newborn son, in the Soignes forest on the outskirts of

Brussels. The trees are straight and high as the ship's masts they were used to build. We are all smiling at the camera, but I can't remember who took this picture.

Postcard. Sepia. A frontier family in front of their soddy. A gaunt and bearded man, his portly wife, and their children—three girls in gingham dresses and a boy in overalls. They are all lined up, the parents seated on chairs in the middle, the girls standing to the left, the boy to the right. There is a cow on the roof, which is also a hillside.

Black-and-white snapshot of my mother and father. They are sitting on a low wall, leaning against each other; they are very young. My mother is wearing a black knit bathing suit. My father is in bathing trunks, without his glasses, thin and smiling. This from some vacation resort in Germany perhaps.

Me sitting in a bath with my brother in Frankfurt, grinning rakishly. I put it on the floor beside me. Shuffling back into the pile on my lap, I find *the empty room in Charlotte.* I put it down beside the bathtub scene. I add *the shadows of the sea birds flying along the beach in North Carolina.* Then I slip all three back into the pile.

A Box of Pictures

A newspaper clipping from the Herald Tribune. The menacing funnel shape of a tornado that ransacked Texas in 1979.

My brother and sisters and I flopped down on the grass with my father in our garden in Vienna. We enjoyed calling ourselves embassy brats, uprooted every two or three years. Berlin, Paris, Frankfurt, Munich, Vienna, Taipei, Paris, Munich, Washington . . . I can hear Dad joking to my mother, "Well, it's been a sort of life . . ."

Outside, I hear my son calling, *"Maman, viens voir!"*

The double doors behind me are slightly ajar and lead directly onto the terrace. I can smell the balmy spring air. But I don't answer right away.

Here is a picture of me at the beach in Cadaqués, just down the coast from the windswept Cap de Creus. My bare back is turned; I am sitting on some rocks looking out to sea.

My son calls again, a little louder, *"Maman!"*

I put all the pictures back into the box, pushing them around gently, sliding their smooth faces against each other as I try to make an even surface of the little paper ocean. So many, I'll never get through everything today. I replace the lid on the box and push it under my desk. I'll need it; I'll just keep it the way it is, here on the floor, next to my feet, a reach away.

I walk out onto our terrace, seeking the expectant voice.